Just like Jasper!

Nick Butterworth and Mick Inkpen

Little, Brown and Company

Boston Toronto London

Jasper is going to the toyshop with his birthday money.

What will he buy?

Will he choose
a ball?

Or perhaps a clockwork mouse?

A noisy drum?

Or some bubbles?

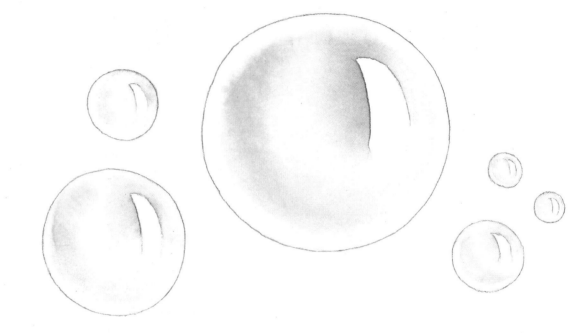

Would he like a car?

Or maybe a doll?

Or a robot?

Will he choose a Jack-in-a-box?

No. Jasper doesn't want any of these.

What has he chosen?

It's a little cat.
Just like Jasper!

First U.S. edition

Library of Congress Catalog Card Number 88-84010

ISBN: 0-316-11917-2

First published in Great Britain by Hodder and Stoughton
Children's Books, a division of Hodder and Stoughton Ltd.,
Mill Road, Dunton Green, Sevenoaks, Kent, TN13 2YJ

10 9 8 7 6 5 4 3 2 1

Printed in Italy